GARFIELD

AND THE

TEACHER CREATURE

Created by Jim Davis
Written by Jim Kraft
Designed and Illustrated by Mike Fentz

Something is wrong, thought Garfield. *I can feel it.*

He rushed into the living room. Jon sat in his chair, moving his lips over the book he was reading. Odie crouched before the spider plant in the corner. Sunlight played on the carpet. Cobwebs stretched across Jon's "Worst Place" bowling trophy. Everything seemed normal.

Suddenly, Garfield knew.

He padded across the room. He stared at four little dents pressed into the carpet.

"Jon," said Garfield.

Jon continued reading.

"Jon, we have to talk."

Still Jon failed to notice his pet.

Grabbing his owner by the ankle, Garfield jerked him out of the chair.

"Garfield! Why did you do that?"

The fat cat pointed to the carpet. "We're missing a major appliance."

"Yes, the TV is gone," said Jon. "I locked it in the closet."

"Why? Was it trying to escape?"

"You were spending too much time watching television," Jon explained. "That's not good for you, Garfield."

"Neither is Odie," replied Garfield, "but you never let me lock *him* in the closet."

"Most television programs are just junk anyway," Jon went on.

"Junk?!" the cat almost yelled. *"Dogs Do the Dumbest Things? Morons on Motorcycles? Smell It and Sell It?* You call that 'junk'?"

"I suppose some TV shows *are* worthwhile," Jon admitted. "Like the 'how-to' ones."

"Exactly," agreed Garfield. "That's where I learned how to wallpaper Odie."

"Even so, I think we'll all be better off this way," Jon concluded as he sat down again.

"We'll all be bored to death this way," grumbled Garfield.

He stomped over to Odie.

"Did you hear?" Garfield asked his friend. "Mr. Entertainment took away our TV."

Odie looked at Garfield with large, unblinking eyes.

"Oh, yeah. Right," muttered Garfield. "Like that matters to you. You just spent six hours watching the spider plant grow."

"By the way, Garfield," Jon said. "I'm taking you and Odie to the vet this afternoon."

Garfield groaned. "Could this day get any worse?"

"She'll probably put you on a diet."

"I had to ask," said Garfield.

"And you'll have to exercise," Jon added.

Garfield sighed. "Might as well. My life is over anyway."

"I think I'll ask Dr. Liz about having you declawed. Then I'll ask her for a date."

"Okay, that's it!" snapped Garfield. "Odie, we're not going to spend one more minute in this TV-hating, vet-loving environment. Pack your bag. We're running away from home."

Odie glanced at Garfield's bulging tummy. He raised an eyebrow.

"Okay, okay. We're *walking* away from home."

Garfield and Odie had barely reached the end of the block when Garfield announced, "Snack break!"

The fat cat flipped open his suitcase. "Let's see what we have," he said. "Cheese, crackers, potato chips, pretzels, candy bars, doughnuts, ice cream, apple pie, cupcakes, cookies, pickles, and peanuts. Oh, and one faithful teddy bear. Glad you came along, Pooky, old pal." He gave the little bear a quick hug.

Frowning, Garfield studied the huge mound of food. "This won't last me through the night," he decided. "Odie, how much food did you bring?"

Odie opened his suitcase. Garfield glanced inside. Odie had packed a rubber bone, a flashlight, and a rock.

"I see you forgot something," said Garfield. "Your *brain*."

"Arf!" replied Odie, nodding his head.

Garfield sighed. "Come on. It'll be getting dark in a few hours. We have to find a place to stay."

Unfortunately, Garfield and Odie were very well known in their neighborhood. No one would let them past the front door.

"I can't believe this," Garfield said indignantly. "You cause one or two minor riots, and the neighbors think you're a troublemaker."

So the two pets kept walking. They came to a part of town where the sidewalks were cracked and the wind swept old newspapers down the streets. MR. SPEEDY DRY-CLEANING, CARTER'S COSTUMES, A-1 HARDWARE—the signs on the empty shops were all old and faded.

Garfield sat down to massage his tired paws. "Odie, I refuse to sleep on the sidewalk. There must be a place for us somewhere." Garfield raised his head. He sniffed the air.

"Ah, someone's boiling pasta," he said dreamily. "According to my nose, the smell is coming from that big building over there."

The abandoned elementary school was a sagging two-story structure with crumbling brick and broken windows. The iron fence was covered with rust.

Weeds had taken over the playground.

Odie whimpered.

"Don't tell me you believe that old story?" said Garfield.

Odie nodded.

Garfield knew the tale. Years ago a new science teacher had come to the school. He was a strange young man,

always talking to himself and jotting formulas in a notebook. Some people thought he was a genius, but others were afraid he was crazy. One day after school he was experimenting with some dangerous chemicals in the science lab. Suddenly a cloud of toxic green gas erupted in his face. He rushed from the classroom and disappeared. They said the accident changed him into a horrible monster—a monster called "the Teacher Creature," a monster who still wandered the lonely corridors of the old school.

"Well, I don't care if the place *is* haunted," Garfield declared. "I'm hungry. Any place that serves pasta is all right with me."

The two pets crossed the street and wriggled through the bars of the fence. When they reached the front door, they found it had been chained shut.

"Do you suppose that's to keep us out," Garfield whispered in a spooky tone, "or to keep the Creature in?"

Odie whined and backed away.

"Oh, stop being a 'fraidy-pup," Garfield told him. "I'm only kidding. That Creature stuff is just a legend. Do you think I'd go near this place if there was really a Creature inside?"

Odie shook his head.

"Of course not," said Garfield. "Now, do you see that broken window? We can climb in through there. You go first."

Odie gave Garfield a long look before clawing his way up the bricks and through the window. Once inside, he leaned out so Garfield could toss the suitcases to him.

Garfield glanced up at the dark,

shattered windows of the school. "It does look a bit creepy," he admitted. Then, muttering, "I don't believe in Creatures, I don't believe in Creatures," he scrambled up after his friend.

Inside the gloomy old building, Garfield and Odie found themselves in a classroom. The rows of wooden desks were long gone, and the chalkboards had been taken away, too. The coatroom was empty, except for a few rusty hooks. Part of a pencil sharpener dangled from the wall.

Garfield sneezed. "I haven't seen this much dust since Jon blew up the vacuum cleaner," he said.

"Ah-choo!" agreed Odie.

"There's so much dust, I can barely smell anything," Garfield complained.

"Although I'm pretty sure that, somewhere around 1955, someone in this room ate a peanut-butter-and-pickle sandwich. Yuck."

Suddenly, the worn floor beneath Garfield began to creak and buckle. "Yikes!" he cried, leaping aside. "This place isn't very safe. We'll have to watch where we step."

Clutching their suitcases, the two pets tiptoed into the hall.

"Awfully quiet in here," Garfield whispered as they made their way down the empty corridors. "I can actually hear the slobber sloshing in your head."

Odie shook his head in reply.

"Please stop," Garfield moaned. "You're making me seasick."

Garfield and Odie stuck their noses into all the classrooms on the first floor. They were all the same: dusty and

deserted. "I smell lots of dirt," said Garfield, "but not a whiff of pasta."

Thump-thump.

"Now I can hear your heart beating," teased Garfield.

Thump-thump.

Garfield looked at Odie. "That *is* your heart beating, isn't it?"

Odie shrugged.

Thump-thump.

"Well, if it's not your heart, and it's not my heart, then what is it?"

Odie spread his arms in a menacing way. He made a ghastly face.

"I told you, the Creature isn't real," said Garfield.

Thump-thump.

"But just in case I'm wrong," Garfield continued, "I suggest that we calmly . . . run for our lives! Last one home is Creature bait!"

They raced to the door at the end of the hall and began pounding on it. But the door wouldn't budge.

Thump-thump.

"Open up, you worthless piece of wood!" Garfield shouted, as he fought with the door handle.

Thump-thump.

The noise was getting closer.

"Odie, we need something thick and heavy to batter down this door. Give me your head."

"Huh?" said Odie.

"Why did you make me run away from home?" Garfield wailed. "I was so happy there!"

"Urf?" said Odie, even more confused than usual.

Thump-thump.

Whatever it was, it would be coming around the corner any second. Garfield grabbed Odie's suitcase and ripped it open.

"Here's the plan," he said. "I'll blind him with the flashlight while you smack him with the rubber bone. And next time, will you please pack some monster spray?"

Odie nodded.

Garfield took Odie's paw. "Old pal, if anything happens to us, there's one thing you should know."

Odie looked at Garfield with tearful eyes.

"It's going to happen to you first," said Garfield. He swung Odie in front of him like a shield and waited for the horrible thing to appear.

Thump-thump.

The Creature drew closer and closer. Garfield and Odie backed against the door.

Thump-thump.

It was nearly there. It was . . . It was . . . Garfield turned on the flashlight.

It was a boy. Startled by the light, he stopped dribbling his basketball, which bounced across the floor.

"Who's there?" asked the boy. He was about ten years old, and he had a backpack slung over his shoulder.

"Odie, you muddle-headed mutt,"

grumbled Garfield. "It's just a kid."

The boy came closer. "I know you guys," he said. "You're Garfield, right?"

"You're honored to meet me, I'm sure," replied Garfield.

"You once hijacked a pizza that was being delivered to my house," the boy said.

"Lies! All lies!" Garfield shouted. "That pizza attacked me. I ate it in self-defense."

"And you're Odie," the boy went on. "People say you're the dumbest dog in the neighborhood."

"Wrong," Garfield argued. "He's the dumbest dog in the universe."

"I'm Andy," the boy told them. "So, what are you guys doing here?" Then he noticed the suitcases. "Oh, I get it. Taking a little time away from home, huh? Well, so am I."

The boy picked up his basketball and began spinning it on his finger.

"You wouldn't believe how my parents treat me. I have to bring in the garbage cans on trash day. I'm not allowed to play video games after supper. And I have to finish my homework before I can shoot hoops. It's like a prison."

"But how's the food?" Garfield asked.

"They even make me eat broccoli," added Andy.

Garfield was horrified. "Oh, you poor child."

"So I thought I'd run away for a few days," Andy explained. "Just to show them I can't be pushed around. I don't really have any place to go, so I guess I'll just hang out here. I know it's not the greatest place. I've heard that Creature story, but I don't believe it."

"Only a dim dog would believe something like that," said Garfield.

"You guys can hang out with me, if you want," Andy offered.

"We'll stay as long as you feed us," Garfield agreed.

Andy dug into his backpack. "I brought all my best stuff. I've got my CD player, hand-held games, comic books, baseball cards, some candy bars—"

Garfield licked his lips. "Now you're talking."

"And the coolest thing of all . . ." From his backpack he drew a wriggling ball of fur. ". . . my hamster, Shermie."

"*Sherman*," squeaked the hamster. "The name is *Sherman*."

"Shermie, say hello to Garfield and Odie."

"I'll do no such thing." Sherman sniffed and turned his head. "I don't associate with common house pets."

"You've got quite an attitude for a rat," observed Garfield.

"Hamster!" Sherman corrected. "And you've got quite an attitude for a fat, furry pumpkin."

"Hey!" exclaimed Garfield.

"Shermie used to work with my dad at the university," Andy told them. "They did experiments together."

"Really," said Garfield. "Like, what makes a hamster explode?"

"Don't be ridiculous," Sherman protested. "I did some very important work in mazes. It was written up in all the scientific journals."

Garfield yawned. "Wow, that's so interesting."

"Of course," Sherman continued, "*you've* never been to the university."

"Cats don't need a university," Garfield declared. "Cats already know everything."

"Oh really?" Sherman replied. "Do you know what 360 times 4,002 equals?"

Garfield thought for a moment. "Well, no," he finally admitted. "Do you?"

"It equals a very large number,"

said Sherman smugly. "If you'd been to a university, you'd know that."

They would have gone on arguing, but suddenly Odie gave a low growl.

"What is it?" asked Andy.

They heard the scrape of footsteps down the hall.

"Someone else is in the building," Andy said nervously. "You don't think it's . . . ?"

"I think it's time to hide," Garfield announced.

They had to find a place quickly. The footsteps were coming nearer. Dropping their bags, the runaways raced down the hall.

"In here!" Garfield ordered. He yanked open a door and leaped inside. Odie, Sherman, and Andy jumped in after him. Andy pulled the door shut.

"I'm scared," Andy whispered.

"I'm squashed," Garfield groaned. "Next time, we hide in separate closets."

Slowly and steadily, the footsteps came closer. Squeezed inside the closet, Garfield, Odie, Andy, and Sherman kept perfectly still.

Suddenly, the footsteps halted . . . right outside the closet!

Garfield started sweating like a polar bear at the beach.

They heard a grunt. Then the footsteps resumed, stopped, started again, and faded away. Somewhere a door opened, the hinges squeaking with age and rust. Then the door slammed shut, and everything was quiet.

Moments later, the closet door burst open. Andy and the pets tumbled into the hall. "That was close," said Andy, sprawled on the floor.

Garfield nodded. "Another minute and we'd have died from hamster breath."

"My breath smells wonderful," the hamster boasted.

"Whatever you say, Vermin," Garfield replied sweetly.

"That's *Sherman!*"

"I don't know who, or what, that was, and I don't really want to find out," Andy declared. "Let's grab our stuff and get out of here."

But when the runaways went to collect their bags, they were gone.

"That 'whatever it was' must have picked up our things," Andy concluded. "At least he didn't take my basketball."

"I still have the flashlight," said Garfield. "All I lost was a few hundred snacks. And Odie can get another rock. They fall out of his head all the time."

"I had all of my best stuff in that backpack," Andy said sadly.

"You still have Vermin," Garfield

pointed out. "Maybe you can trade him to the Creature for your more valuable possesions."

"To quote Albert Einstein," said Sherman, "'You stink, and so do your relatives.'"

"Einstein never said that," argued Garfield.

"Did too," insisted Sherman. "It's in his theory of relativity."

Andy made a decision.

"Garfield and Odie, *you* should probably get out of here. But I can't go home yet. My parents will just make me do the same things all over again. Heck, they'll probably give me more chores because I ran away. Besides, I have to get my stuff back."

"Are you crazy, kid?" Garfield exclaimed. "The Creature could be lurking around the next corner. You'll never make it out of here alive."

"Does the term 'scaredy cat' mean anything to you?" asked Sherman.

"Does 'hamster burger' mean anything to you?" Garfield responded.

"Catch you later, guys," Andy said. "Good luck." Scooping up his hamster and his basketball, the boy turned and walked away down the hall.

"Scaredy cat, scaredy cat . . . "
Sherman squeaked.

Garfield watched them fade into the shadows. "I'm not risking my fur for a few doughnuts," he said to Odie. "Let's get out of here."

Suddenly, a look of horror came over Garfield's face. "Pooky!" he cried. "That monster has my Pooky!" He turned to Odie. "Well? What are you waiting for? Go find the Creature!"

It was night. The boy and the pets walked cautiously through the dark hallways, guided by the beam from Garfield's flashlight.

"This reminds me of the last time Jon changed a lightbulb," Garfield recalled. "It took the electric company three days to get the power back on."

A startled rat skittered across the floor, making them all jump.

"One of your cousins?" Garfield asked Sherman.

The hamster glared at Garfield.

"Let's find a safe place to sleep,"

Andy suggested. "We can look for our things tomorrow."

The beam of light revealed a door. Beyond it was a large room with a high ceiling and tall windows on two sides. Light from the streetlamps outside filtered through the grimy glass.

"Must be the old gym," said Andy. "Hey, look!"

At the far end of the room, a basketball hoop still hung from a wooden backboard.

Andy dribbled toward it. On the run, he flipped the ball off the backboard and through the basket.

"He shoots! He scores!" Andy roared.

Andy launched shot after shot at the basket, while Garfield aimed the flashlight for him.

"This is great!" Andy exclaimed.

"I've always dreamed of having my own gym. Do you guys want to shoot some?"

"No, thanks," Garfield replied. "Exercise is bad for my shape."

But Odie barked enthusiastically.

"Here, boy," said Andy. "I'll bounce the ball off the floor, and you jump up and hit it into the basket with your nose. I saw a dog do that in a movie."

"This should be disastrous," warned Garfield.

Andy bounced the ball on the floor. Odie leaped and butted the ball with his head. The ball banked off Andy's head,

clanged against the rim of the hoop, rocketed downward, ricocheted off Garfield's face, looped high into the air, and dropped through the goal.

"Nice shot, Odie," groaned Andy, rubbing his head.

Garfield picked himself up off the floor. "Someday I'm gonna slam dunk that dog," he muttered.

Andy resumed dribbling and shooting.

"Good thing I ran away," he said. "Do you know what I'd be doing at home right now? Homework. Or taking a bath. I wouldn't be having fun like this."

"I wouldn't be having fun like this, either," Garfield complained. "I'd be having fun that was fun."

"I'm sure your little home is quite amusing," said Sherman.

"It's not so bad," Garfield told him. "I've got a bed to sleep in, a teddy bear to hug, a refrigerator to empty, an owner to annoy, and a dog to wallpaper. Actually, it's a pretty good place to be."

"Sounds extremely stimulating," Sherman commented sarcastically.

"Okay, so it's not the university,"
Garfield said. "But at least we don't
have any monsters." He pointed with the
flashlight. "Like that one, for instance."

Sherman gave a squeak of alarm.
Garfield's eyes bulged. Andy and Odie
gasped.

There, in the glow of Garfield's
light, stood the Teacher Creature! It was

about six feet tall and dressed in ragged clothes and worn-out boots. Its scaly green hands ended in long, sharp claws. Its face looked barely human.

Garfield smiled nervously at the monster. "You know," he said, "not everyone could wear an outfit like that. But the mutant look really works for you."

The Creature came toward them, its feet scraping across the floor. The runaways were too frightened to move.

Suddenly, Garfield grabbed for Sherman. Pointing the terrified rodent at the monster, he shouted, "Freeze, Slimeface! I've got a hamster here, and I'm not afraid to use it!"

The Creature halted.

"Let me go!" squealed Sherman.

"No way," Garfield growled. "I've got more to live for than you do. Tomorrow night's two-for-one at the pizza parlor."

At that moment, Andy hurled his basketball at the distracted monster. "Oof," the Creature grunted as the ball hit him in the stomach.

"Run!" Andy shouted.

Garfield dropped the hamster, and they all took off in different directions.

Driven by fear, Garfield raced through the halls like an orange meteorite. He ran in circles. He ran in squares. He ran up stairs and down. Finally, he stumbled into a room and collapsed on the floor, his heart pounding like an elephant skipping rope.

"I can hear the news report now," Garfield gasped. "Sweaty cat mauled by monster. Film at eleven."

It was some time before the fat cat was able to sit up and wave his flashlight around.

"I must . . . be in the basement," panted Garfield. A huge old furnace squatted in the middle of the room, its pipes stretching far into the corners of the school like the arms of a giant spider.

Hmmm, Garfield said to himself. *Something smells familiar.* He followed his nose to the furnace. Opening the steel door, he saw a worn, dented cooking pot with noodles stuck to the bottom. *What do you know?* he thought. *The Creature likes macaroni.*

Garfield squeezed around the side of the furnace. Behind it was a space crammed with all kinds of things: a pile of old clothes; cardboard boxes; candles and matches on a small wooden table; plastic plates and cups; dirty blankets on the floor. And . . . a werewolf in the corner.

"Yikes!" cried Garfield. The beam
of his flashlight shone on the face of a
snarling monster.

"Don't eat me!" begged the
petrified pet. "I'm loaded with sugar.
Your fangs will fall out."

Instead of pouncing on the
helpless cat, the werewolf just stared

in sinister silence. Garfield looked more closely.

It wasn't a real werewolf at all. It was a rubber mask propped on top of some boxes. Garfield picked up the mask, turning it in the light.

Things are getting stranger and stranger, he thought. Just then, his flashlight beam revealed something else.

"Our stuff!" said Garfield out loud. Andy's backpack and the suitcases had been tossed in another corner.

Garfield ripped open his suitcase. "Pooky! You're all right!" He hugged the teddy bear tightly. "I was afraid you'd become a monster meal.

"And that reminds me—I'm starving," Garfield said. "I'm sure Andy won't mind if I borrow a candy bar." He plunged his paw into Andy's backpack.

"Yeow!" he squealed as something sharp dug into his thumb. He dropped the backpack and aimed the flashlight at it. Two little eyes stared back at him.

"Vermin!" snarled Garfield. "How did you get here?"

"Hamsters have an excellent sense of smell," Sherman explained, as he nibbled a candy bar.

"Why did you bite me?"

"I felt threatened," Sherman said.

"You'll feel flattened, if you don't give me that candy bar."

The hamster handed over the snack. Garfield gobbled it down in one bite.

"When I was at the university," Sherman began, "we did an experiment where—"

"Sorry, boring time is over," Garfield announced, stuffing Sherman back in the bag and zipping it shut. "We've got to get out of here."

Struggling with the backpack, the two suitcases, the flashlight, and Pooky, Garfield made his way slowly through the halls. He peeked around every corner, alert for any sign of the Creature. But the corridors were empty and still. Finally, he found the gym.

Andy's basketball lay on the floor

where it had bounced off the Creature.

"Odie . . . ? Andy . . . ?" Garfield called softly.

There was no answer.

Garfield let Sherman out of the backpack. "I feel certain they got away," the hamster said.

"I hope you're right," Garfield answered. "But we can't look for them anymore tonight. If I don't get some sleep, my eyeballs will fall out. I'm taking this part of the floor. You can sleep wherever you like."

Garfield opened his suitcase. "It's not a bed," he said, squeezing Pooky and himself into the bottom of the case, "but it's not bad. Good night, Pooky. Good to have you back." Garfield shut his eyes.

Two minutes later, he felt a tap on the nose.

"What is it, Vermin?" he mumbled.

"Uh, would you mind terribly if I joined you?" the hamster asked.

"This bed is full."

"Otherwise I'll keep you awake by talking all night," Sherman said.

Garfield rolled his eyes. "Get in," he sighed. "But don't touch the teddy bear."

Sherman squeezed into the suitcase next to Garfield and Pooky. Soon the cat and the hamster were snoring away.

Garfield yawned and rubbed his eyes. "What a night," he said. "I had this terrible dream. The Creature had captured me, and he kept poking me in the side with his claws."

"I was trying to make you roll over," said Sherman. "Your snoring was horrible."

"Thank you," Garfield replied.

"You probably have sinus snore-itis," Sherman stated.

"What?" said Garfield.

"It's a standard medical term," the hamster told him.

"How would *you* know?" Garfield shot back. "You're not a doctor."

"I did some research at the university hospital," Sherman declared proudly. "My cage was lined with old medical reports."

They were interrupted by a shower of plaster dust and the sound of footsteps racing across the roof above the gym.

"That reminds me," Sherman continued, as he brushed the dust from his whiskers. "The ceiling of the Sistine Chapel in Rome is—"

"Hold the lecture, Vermin!" said Garfield. "Don't you hear that barking? There's trouble on the roof. We need to get up there right away!"

Garfield and Sherman dashed upstairs. They could hear Andy yelling and Odie barking angrily.

"Hang on, old buddy!" Garfield called, as he bravely threw open a door.

The Creature stood hunched in the middle of the roof, his arms wrapped tightly around Andy. "Let me go, you big green freak!" the boy hollered.

"Get your claws off that kid!" cried Garfield. Racing across the roof, he hurled himself onto the Creature's back. At the same time, Odie sank his teeth into its ankle. The monster let out a howl.

"I'll teach you to terrorize my teddy bear!" shouted Garfield, tugging fiercely on the Creature's ears. To Garfield's amazement, its head came off!

"Boy, they don't make monsters like they used to," the fat cat said, gazing at the floppy rubber face in his paws.

"Call off your pets, will ya, kid? I promise not to hurt you."

Andy stopped kicking. He looked up. "Hey!" he said. "You're not the Creature. You're just an ordinary guy!"

"What are you doing here?" asked the man. "Don't you know this building isn't safe?"

"Who are you?" Andy demanded.

"And what have you done with the Teacher Creature?" Garfield added.

"Later," said the man. "We need to get off this roof before it collapses. This cat weighs a ton."

"I liked you better as a monster," snapped Garfield.

Then, with a cracking roar, the roof caved in.

Four frightened figures swung high above the gym floor.

The man dressed like a monster dangled from the end of a splintered beam, hanging on by the tips of a single costumed hand. With his other hand, the man clutched Andy, who grabbed on to Garfield, who held tight to Odie.

Sherman, still on the roof, peered down at them.

"Tsk, tsk," said the hamster. "This is a problem."

"Thanks for the news bulletin," Garfield muttered.

"If I estimate your weight correctly," the hamster continued, "and factor in wind resistance, the velocity at which you'll hit the floor should be . . ."

"Should be what?" asked Garfield.

"Should be enough to cause a major boo-boo."

"Stop thinking and get some help!" Garfield ordered.

"I'm afraid there isn't time for that," Sherman replied.

"I can't hold on much longer," grunted the man through gritted teeth.

"What did I tell you?" said Sherman.

"Vermin, when I get out of the hospital, you're going to be one sorry rodent," Garfield warned.

The hamster looked quickly around the roof. "I may have a solution," he said. "Hold on."

"That's exactly what we're doing," Garfield reminded him.

"My hands are slipping!" cried Andy.

"Don't let go!" pleaded Garfield. He looked down at Odie. "Old pal," he said, "before we fall, there's one thing I want you to know."

Odie gazed tenderly at Garfield.

"If you land on Pooky, I'll pulverize you."

"Grrr," said Odie, scowling.

Then they heard a clanking noise, followed by hamster squeaks, and the sound of something being dragged across the shattered roof.

Sherman's face reappeared at the edge of the hole in the gym ceiling. In his paws he held the nozzle of a fire hose.

"Whew!" he puffed. "That was very

difficult. It's a lucky thing they left the emergency fire hose on the roof."

"Very lucky," said Garfield, "except that we're not on fire."

"I know that. I'm going to drop one end of this hose onto the gym floor. The other end is attached to the chimney. That way, you can simply slide down to safety."

Sherman tossed the hose through the hole.

"Ouch!" Garfield grumbled as the heavy nozzle banged into his head.

"I'm sorry," said Sherman. "Your head is bigger than I thought."

Slowly and carefully, Garfield, Odie, Andy, and the man let go of each other and grabbed on to the fire hose. One by one, they slid down the hose until they landed safely on the floor.

"Shermie, you saved us," Andy exclaimed when the hamster joined them in the gym. "You're a hero." He gave the little animal a big hug.

"We owe you one, Vermin," said Garfield.

"Well, you were quite brave when you tried to rescue Andy from the Creature," Sherman acknowledged.

"Thank you, Vermin. I mean, *Sherman.*"

"Although you could lose some weight," the hamster concluded.

"Don't push it," said Garfield.

When they had all recovered from their scary experience, Ted (for that was the man's name) told them his story.

"I owned the costume shop across the street," he began. "It used to be a good little business. Then the school closed, and the neighborhood went bad. I did everything I could to save the store, but it was no use. I was so far in debt that I lost the store and my home. I had no money and no place to go. So I thought I'd stay here for a while."

"Why were you pretending to be the Teacher Creature?" Andy asked.

EXIT

The man shrugged. "I didn't want anyone to find me. I had a few costume pieces left from the store, and I'd heard stories about the monster. I thought the best way to keep the neighborhood kids away from here would be to scare them."

"You scared the neighborhood pets, too," Garfield commented.

"You're lucky to live here," said Andy. He told the stranger about the rules he had to follow at home.

"Our place is even worse," Garfield chimed in. "Besides, you should smell Jon's dirty socks."

"Maybe we could all stay here with you," Andy suggested. "We could all be the Teacher Creature."

Ted thought it over for a moment. "All right," he agreed. "But you'll have to follow the rules."

"Rules?" said Andy.

"Every place has rules, kid. The first rule here is: no basketball."

"No basketball!"

"All that thumping gives me a headache," Ted explained. "Besides, it interferes with your homework."

"Homework?" asked Andy.

"Sure," Ted answered. "You have to go to school. That's another rule."

"Anything else?" said Andy sadly.

"No pets."

"Cancel my reservation," Garfield decided.

Frowning, Andy twirled his basketball on his finger. "I guess I might as well go home then," he sighed.

"You might as well, kid," Ted replied.

"But we'll visit you," Andy offered.

The man shook his head. "This place is too dangerous, even for me."

"What will you do?" asked the boy.

"I'm moving."

"Where to?"

"California," Ted said. "I got in touch with a friend. He says he has a job for me in the movie-costume business."

A short time later, Garfield, Odie, and Andy paused outside the iron fence surrounding the old school building. Andy bounced his basketball. Sherman peeked out of the backpack. They waved one last time to Ted, who raised his hand before slipping into the shadows.

The runaways started home. Garfield carried his suitcase, with Pooky safe inside. Soon it was time for Andy to turn off toward his house.

"It was fun hanging out with you guys," he told Garfield and Odie. "Maybe I'll see you around the neighborhood."

"And maybe I won't," squeaked Sherman.

"Hang in there, Andy," Garfield said encouragingly. "Maybe someday you'll get a real pet instead of a know-it-all fur ball."

Sherman stuck out his tongue, then ducked his head inside the pack. Andy waved and marched away.

It wasn't long before the two pets were back at Jon's house.

"Garfield! Odie!" cried Jon, giving them a big hug. "Where have you been?

I've been worried about you."

"We went to night school," said Garfield.

"You must be starving," Jon declared. "Come on, let's get some food. Then we'll all do something fun together. *I* know! You can help me sort my toothpick collection!"

Garfield smiled. *Be it ever so boring*, he thought, *there's no place like home.*

About Garfield's Creator

Jim Davis is the award-winning creator of Garfield. He is the only author to have seven books appear simultaneously on the *New York Times* best-seller list.

Jim lives in Indiana. His hobbies include golf, fishing, and eating jelly doughnuts. An active environmentalist, Jim dreams of the day when there will be a cure for dog breath.

About the Author

Jim Kraft was a classics major at Kenyon College. Finding the market for Roman historians to be a tad depressed, he naturally turned to greeting card writing. Eventually he started writing for Garfield. He is the author of more than 60 children's books and several really snappy postcards.

Mr. Kraft lives in Carmel, Indiana, with his wife, two sons, and six basketballs.

About the Illustrator

Mike Fentz attended Herron School of Art in Indianapolis. After spending ten years crisscrossing the country as a caricaturist, Mike joined Paws, Inc. (the Garfield company), where he works as an artist, designing and illustrating children's books.

Mike lives in Muncie, Indiana, with his wife and two daughters. An avid runner, he hopes to compete in the Boston Marathon before he develops cataracts on his knees.